DINK, JOSH, AND RUTH ROSE AREN'T THE
ONLY KID DETECTIVES!

WHAT ABOUT YOU?

CAN YOU FIND THE HIDDEN MESSAGE
INSIDE THIS BOOK?

There are 26 illustrations in this book, not counting the one on the title page, the map at the beginning, and the picture of a leopard that repeats at the start of many of the chapters. In each of the 26 illustrations, there's a hidden letter. If you can find all the letters, you will spell out a secret message!

If you're stumped, the answer is on the bottom of page 135.

HAPPY DETECTING!

This book is dedicated to Ben Hancock—teacher, mentor, friend.
—R.R.

To Nolan and Colby
—J.S.G.

Text copyright © 2022 by Ron Roy
Cover art copyright © 2022 by Stephen Gilpin
Interior illustrations copyright © 2022 by John Steven Gurney

Many thanks to Shannon Seglin of the San Antonio Public Library for compiling the list of titles for further reading on pages 137–138.

Visit us on the Web!
rhcbooks.com

Educators and librarians, for a variety of teaching tools,
visit us at RHTeachersLibrarians.com

Library of Congress Cataloging-in-Publication Data
Names: Roy, Ron, author. | Gurney, John Steven, illustrator.
Title: Leopard on the loose / by Ron Roy; illustrated by John Steven Gurney.
Description: New York: Random House Children's Books, [2022] | Series: A to Z
mysteries super edition; 14 | "A Stepping Stone book" | Includes bibliographical
references. | Audience: Ages 6–9. | Summary: "When a leopard goes missing at the San
Diego Zoo, it's up to Dink, Josh, and Ruth Rose to find her!"—Provided by publisher.
Identifiers: LCCN 2021005066 (print) | LCCN 2021005067 (ebook) |
ISBN 978-0-593-30184-5 (trade paperback) | ISBN 978-0-593-30185-2 (library binding) |
ISBN 978-0-593-30186-9 (ebook)
Subjects: CYAC: Zoos—Fiction. | Zoo animals—Fiction. | Mystery and detective stories.
Classification: LCC PZ7.R8139 Le 2022 (print) | LCC PZ7.R8139 (ebook) |
DDC [Fic]—dc23

Printed in the United States of America
10 9 8 7 6 5 4 3 2 1

This book has been officially leveled by using the F&P Text Level Gradient™
Leveling System.

Random House Children's Books supports the First Amendment and celebrates the right to read.

A to Z Mysteries®

SUPER EDITION 14

Leopard on the Loose

by Ron Roy

illustrated by
John Steven Gurney

A STEPPING STONE BOOK™

Random House New York

CHAPTER ONE

"Guys, she's looking right at me!" Josh whispered. "I'm face-to-face with a leopard!"

Dink and his friends Josh and Ruth Rose were at the San Diego Zoo, in California. They were standing outside a walled enclosure. On the other side of the wall was Jade, an Amur leopard.

Josh leaned against the short concrete wall. The concrete was painted gray, brown, and green to look like boulders. On top of the concrete wall was wire fencing, fifteen feet tall and twenty feet wide. People who wanted to look inside Jade's enclosure could see easily through the wire.

Inside the enclosure, Jade dozed on a boulder in the late-evening sun. She made a soft coughing noise in her throat. Her long, thick tail flicked back and forth, keeping flies away.

"I think she likes you," Dink said.

"I wonder why they named her Jade," Josh said.

"Because her eyes are jade green," Ruth Rose said. "Like your eyes, too. And like my outfit."

Ruth Rose liked to dress all in one color so that everything matched. Today's color was green, from her sneakers to her headband. Dink and Josh wore shorts and T-shirts.

Ruth Rose read from a plaque attached to the wall. "Amur leopards are from Russia and China," she told Dink

and Josh. "There are only about a hundred left in the wild!"

"That is so sad!" Josh said. "What if they all die?"

"Zoos like this one try to breed more leopards," Dink said.

"Jade was born in this zoo three years ago," Ruth Rose added. "And now she's expecting her first baby!"

"Awesome!" Josh said. The three kids peered at her through the fencing. Her enclosure looked like a forest. Boulders were stacked so she could climb, with a space underneath that formed a cave. Trees and shrubbery grew among rocks. There was a small pond where Jade could get a drink or take a swim.

Dink, Josh, and Ruth Rose were at the zoo with their friend Parker Stone. He was fifteen and had his own TV show, *Roger to the Rescue*. In the show, Parker played Roger Good, a teenager who traveled around the world helping animals.

A new episode of *Roger to the Rescue* would be about Amur leopards, and Parker had invited Dink, Josh, and Ruth Rose to appear on the show with him. Last year, the kids had rescued Parker from kidnappers near the Grand Canyon.

Watching Jade with the kids and Parker were Sparky Carson, the show's videographer, and Debbie Jones, the producer.

Jade stood and stretched, lashing her tail. She yawned, showing long white teeth, then let out a soft bark and lay back down. She licked her plump belly.

"Jade looks like she could have her baby at any time," Debbie said. "Are you getting this on film, Sparky?"

"Got it," Sparky said, aiming his camera.

Just then, a golf cart zoomed up to the wall. The driver was a man with brown hair, wearing a dark-blue shirt. In the passenger seat was Dr. Akbar, the zoo's head veterinarian.

Dr. Akbar hopped out. "Thanks for the ride, Rob," he told the driver. "I'll bring the cart back to the maintenance shed later."

Rob nodded and walked away.

"Hi, Dr. Akbar," Parker said.

"Hey, folks," the vet said. "Did I miss anything?"

"Jade just yawned at us," Parker said.

"After that, she licked her belly."

Dr. Akbar grinned. "That's my girl," he said. Then he approached the wall and said, "I brought you a treat!"

He pulled a baggie from his vest pocket.

"What's the treat?" Josh asked.

Dr. Akbar held up the baggie. "Power meatballs," he said.

"What makes them powerful?" Josh asked.

"When the kitchen staff makes the meatballs, they tuck some special vitamins inside," Dr. Akbar explained. "Jade will get her vitamins without even knowing it."

He opened the bag and tossed two meatballs high over the wire fencing. They landed a few feet in front of Jade. She bounded from her boulder to sniff the meatballs. Then she gobbled them down, licked her lips, and walked into her cave.

"I guess we're done filming for tonight," Debbie said. "Let's pack up, Sparky."

"The zoo is closing," Dr. Akbar said. "I'll come back tomorrow to see if she gave birth overnight."

"I was really looking forward to seeing a baby leopard," Ruth Rose said.

"We all were," Debbie said. "This whole episode is supposed to be Parker telling his viewers about endangered animals, especially Amur leopards. Getting this new cub into the show would help Parker's message."

"Can you come back tomorrow?" Dr. Akbar asked.

"We'll be here," Debbie said. "Kids, I'll pick you and Parker up around eight, okay?"

"So I'll see you all then," Dr. Akbar said. He drove the cart down the path, toward an exit gate.

Everyone else got into a larger cart

the zoo had lent to Parker's team. This one was bright green with a white canvas top and three rows of seats. It was nicknamed "the Bug."

Debbie got behind the wheel, and Parker took the front passenger seat. Dink, Josh, and Ruth Rose sat behind them. Sparky took the backseat, where there was room for him and his equipment.

"Can I drive?" Parker asked, grinning at Debbie.

"Sure, when you're sixteen," Debbie said. She steered the Bug along a wide path usually crowded with zoo visitors. The path was empty and quiet now.

"But I know how," Parker said. "My parents let me practice driving in our neighborhood so I can get my learner's permit."

"Your parents aren't here," Debbie said. "I am, so for now we go with my rules."

She drove out through the zoo's front gates, passing the giant lion sculpture that greeted zoo visitors. Then she steered the Bug through the empty parking lot, toward three trailers in a row.

Parker hopped out of the Bug. "See you tomorrow," he said. "Got homework to do."

"You have homework?" Josh said. "But you've got your own TV show!"

"It's an assignment for my writing class," Parker said. "I'm writing a story. If my teacher likes it, we may make a movie out of it next year."

"What's the story about?" Ruth Rose asked.

Parker grinned. "About how I got kidnapped last year and you guys saved me," he said. "I'm at the part where I was tied up under that cabin floor."

"If they make the movie," Josh asked, "will we be in it?"

Parker shook his head. "They'll hire some actor kids," he said.

"Bummer," Josh said.

Debbie moved the Bug to Sparky's trailer. He hauled his equipment off the rear seats and carried it into his trailer. Debbie moved the Bug to the front of her trailer and parked it next to a blue van. She and the kids climbed into the van, and Debbie headed out of the parking lot and turned left.

It was getting dark, and the trees and benches they passed cast shadows onto the road.

"It's pretty here," Ruth Rose said as the van passed a small pond.

"Are we still in the zoo?" Dink asked.

Debbie shook her head. "No, we're driving through Balboa Park now," she said. "The zoo is part of Balboa Park, which is about 150 years old. Back in 1916, the city gave permission to open the zoo on park grounds."

"So is our motel in Balboa Park, too?" Dink asked.

"No, the Zoo-Tel is just outside the park," Debbie said.

Suddenly something flew over their heads. It made a whirring noise before it disappeared.

CHAPTER TWO

"What was that?" Josh asked. "A vampire bat?"

"Actually, it looked like a drone," Debbie said. "It had lights."

"Why would anyone fly a drone now? It's almost dark," Dink said.

"That's why drones have lights," Debbie said. "Plus, some carry tiny cameras so the owners can film stuff they fly over. Drones can make deliveries, too. They can bring a small package right to your house."

"If I had one, I'd teach it to bring me cheeseburgers!" Josh said.

"How far is it to our motel?" Ruth Rose asked.

"A couple of miles," Debbie said. "We're leaving Balboa Park now." She pointed to a sign that said THANKS FOR VISITING BALBOA PARK. COME BACK SOON!

The van cruised past a small building among some bushes on the right side of the road.

"What's that place?" Josh asked.

"I think it used to be a home for some of the workers who developed the park a long time ago," Debbie said. "Now it's just empty, I guess."

"How come there are no other houses around here?" Josh asked.

"The city doesn't allow homes in Balboa Park," Debbie said.

"I wouldn't want to live down the road from a zoo," Josh said. "If a tiger got loose, it could climb in through my bedroom window!"

Ten minutes later, they arrived at

the Zoo-Tel, where the kids and Dink's father were staying. Debbie stopped the van next to Mr. Duncan's rental car.

Dink's dad stepped out of room 10. "Welcome home!" he said. "Do we have a baby leopard yet?"

"Afraid not," Debbie said. "We're going to try again tomorrow morning. Okay to pick the kids up around eight?"

"Perfect," Dink's father said. "Thank you."

"No problem, Mr. Duncan." Debbie waved and headed back to the road.

"Can we go in the pool, Dad?" Dink asked.

"No, sorry. I have pizza for you," his father said. "How about a swim tomorrow morning before Debbie picks you up?"

"Awesome, Mr. Duncan!" Josh said. Mr. Duncan led the kids to room 10.

The Zoo-Tel was shaped like a horse-shoe. There were fourteen guest rooms, all facing a swimming pool in the center.

Dink's father had reserved three rooms: one for himself, one for Dink and Josh to share, and one for Ruth Rose. On one side of the pool, a café named Goodies sold snacks.

Each room at the Zoo-Tel had been given a different animal theme. Room 10 had a gorilla face painted on the door, and one wall inside was painted to resemble a jungle. Parrots, monkeys, and other creatures peeked out from the foliage.

"Thanks for the pizza, Dad," Dink said, wiping his mouth with a paper napkin. "How'd you know we'd be starving?"

His father laughed. "Just a guess," he said. "So tell me about Jade."

"She's beautiful," Dink said.

"She has green eyes like mine!" Josh said.

"And her fur is golden with brown spots," Ruth Rose added.

"Sadly, that beautiful fur is the main reason Amur leopards are nearly extinct,"

Mr. Duncan said. "Poachers kill them and sell the skins to people who make fur coats."

"That is so disgusting!" Ruth Rose said.

"It is," Mr. Duncan said. "But zoos like the one here in San Diego are trying to help. And there are organizations trying to train poachers for other jobs so they don't have to kill animals to make money."

"What kinds of organizations?" Dink asked his father.

"I'll go online and let you know what I find," his father answered.

They finished the pizza.

"I'll wake you at seven for a swim," Dink's father said.

"What about breakfast?" Josh asked. "I'll be starving by then!"

"I'm on it," Mr. Duncan told him. "Now off to bed."

CHAPTER THREE

Dink woke up to knocking at the door. "Wakey-wakey!" his father's voice called. "It's Dad."

Dink jumped out of bed and opened the door. His father was holding four small paper bags that smelled delicious.

Mr. Duncan handed Dink three of the bags. "I'm going next door to eat and enjoy my coffee," he said. "I'll knock on Ruth Rose's door and tell her to come over here."

"Can we still go swimming?" Dink asked.

"Sure, if you hurry."

The kids ate, changed into swimsuits, and ran out to the pool. They plunged in, nearly wetting Dink's father, who was sitting outside his door reading a newspaper.

After fifteen minutes of swimming, Dink's father called them out and handed them towels. They dried off and went back to the rooms to change just as Debbie drove up. Parker sat next to her, and Sparky was in the rear seat of the van with all his equipment.

"Can you have them back around noon?" Dink's father asked Debbie once the kids were all ready.

"Sure," Debbie said. "We're just going to do a thirty-minute shoot of the leopard and Dr. Akbar, the vet. We'll add Parker's voice later."

"Great. See you soon, kids," Mr. Duncan said. "Have fun!"

"Bye!" the kids called, and climbed into the van.

"How's your story coming along?" Dink asked Parker.

"Pretty slow," Parker said. "I get scared again, thinking about spiders crawling over me when I—"

"Stop!" Josh said. "Let's think happy thoughts!"

"Here's a happy thought," Ruth Rose said. "I dreamed that Jade had her baby!"

"I hope your dream comes true," Debbie said. "A new baby Amur leopard could be a very big deal for my show."

After they arrived at the zoo, Debbie drove the kids in the Bug over to Jade's enclosure. As she was parking, Dr. Akbar was pacing in front of the wall with his cell phone pressed against one ear.

"I don't *know*!" he shouted. "Jade's not in her enclosure. I just got here, and she's gone! She must have escaped somehow. She's pregnant and probably fearful for her cub. So don't let any visitors in. I doubt she'd leave the zoo, but call the TV stations so they can alert anyone in Balboa Park!"

"Oh my gosh!" Josh said. "There's a leopard on the loose!"

Dr. Akbar walked over to the Bug. "Jade's escaped," he told them. His face was sweaty, and his eyes were red. "I've told the zoo manager. No one is allowed in, and I'm afraid you won't be able to film today, Ms. Jones."

Debbie stared at him. "Is she . . . are we in danger?" she asked.

"I don't think so," Dr. Akbar said.

"Jade is pretty shy. Most likely, she's hiding nearby on the zoo grounds, probably sleeping. She'd never attack anyone."

The kids climbed out of the Bug and peered through the wire fencing.

"Now what am I supposed to do?" Debbie mumbled. "I need this footage!"

Holding on to the wire fencing, Dink bent over and tried to peer into Jade's cave. The inside was dark, so he wouldn't have been able to spot Jade even if she were there. When he stood up, he felt something wet on the palm of his right hand.

It was black and sticky. Dink took a sniff, then wiped his hand on the back of his shorts. He looked at the fencing where he'd placed his hands.

"How could Jade get out?" Ruth Rose asked Dr. Akbar. "This wall is really tall!"

"Around fifteen feet high," Dr. Akbar said. "Leopards are good climbers, so the wall was built leaning in. No animal should be able to get over it."

Sparky set his equipment on the ground. "What do you want to do?" he asked Debbie.

"Shoot the enclosure anyway," Debbie said. "And be sure to get shots of the empty cave. I want the whole thing—the pond, the wall, get it all!"

"You want me in this?" Parker asked.

"Yes! Sparky, get some footage of Parker looking unhappy," Debbie said.

Parker posed, and Sparky got him on film.

"Are you sure Jade's not just hiding in her cave?" Ruth Rose asked Dr. Akbar.

"We have a camera in there," Dr. Akbar said. "The cave is empty."

"So if she got out, where would she go?" Dink asked.

"Jade was born here," he said. "She's used to these sounds and smells, so I'm guessing she'd stay here on the grounds."

Josh stepped closer to the Bug. "You

mean she could be, like, watching us?" he whispered.

"Don't worry. I should be able to coax Jade back," Dr. Akbar said. "When she was younger, I played with her a lot and took her for walks. She knows I'm her friend."

"Yeah, but she doesn't know me!" Josh said.

"Has Jade tried to escape before?" Dink asked.

"No, but animals behave differently when they're about to give birth," Dr. Akbar said. "If Jade saw or heard something that she thought was a threat, she might've decided to find a new place to have her cub."

"We're leaving," Debbie announced. "Come on, everyone, pack up."

"Sorry about your show, Ms. Jones," Dr. Akbar said.

Debbie nodded. "Me too," she said.

CHAPTER FOUR

"Dr. Akbar, if the wall is too steep to climb," Josh asked, "how did Jade get out?"

"I have one idea," Dr. Akbar said. He led the kids along the outside of the enclosure. He stopped and pointed to a tree growing just inside the wall.

"This oak tree is about thirty feet tall," he said. "See how that branch hangs over the wall? Jade could've climbed the tree, crawled onto the branch, and leaped to the ground."

Dink looked at his watch. It was almost nine o'clock. "When do you think she got out?" he asked.

"During the night," Dr. Akbar said. "I already spoke to the guards who were patrolling. They said they didn't see or hear anything unusual."

Ruth Rose looked at Dink and Josh. "Remember that drone we saw last night?" she asked. "Maybe that's what scared her!"

"You saw a drone?" Dr. Akbar asked. "Where?"

"It flew over us when Debbie was driving us to the Zoo-Tel," Josh said. "It was flying real low, and it had lights and made a buzzing noise. Maybe it came over the enclosure and Jade saw it."

"That could have frightened her," Dr. Akbar said. "Anyway, I've got to meet with the zoo director."

He jumped into his cart and sped away. The kids walked over to Parker and Debbie.

"Let's load up," Debbie said. She helped Sparky put his equipment on the

Bug's rear seat. "Parker? Kids? Ready to go?"

Parker sat next to Debbie, and the kids climbed in behind them. As Debbie headed toward the exit, Dink, Josh, and Ruth Rose watched the bushes for green eyes looking back at them.

Outside the zoo's gates, Debbie drove to the far side of the empty parking lot. The Bug's tires splashed through a few puddles. Sparky hopped off and took his equipment into his trailer.

Parker got out, too. "Back to my story," he muttered.

"Does it have a title?" Dink asked.

"Yeah," Parker said. "I'm calling it 'Grand Canyon Grab.'"

"Because the bad guys grabbed you at the Grand Canyon!" Josh said.

Parker grinned. "I hope my teacher likes it," he said. He fist-bumped the kids and walked to his trailer.

After Debbie and the kids switched

to the van, she drove out the exit gate and turned left along one of Balboa Park's shady roads.

She glanced at the kids. "Next stop, the Zoo-Tel," she said. "Your dad will be surprised to see you back so soon!"

"Um, we've decided to explore Balboa Park," Dink announced.

"We have?" Josh asked. "When—"

Dink nudged Josh with his elbow. "My dad will be working now anyway," he went on.

"But how will you get back to the Zoo-Tel?" Debbie asked. "It's at least three miles from here."

"I'll text my dad, and he'll pick us up," Dink said.

"At noon?" Debbie asked. "That's three hours from now!"

Dink grinned. "Yeah, we really like to explore new places!"

"Well, if you're sure," Debbie said. She pulled over and stopped. "Have fun!"

The kids climbed out of the van and watched Debbie drive away.

"Okay, what's going on?" Josh asked.

"Yeah, Dink, what's up?" Ruth Rose asked.

"Something weird," Dink said.

"What?" Ruth Rose asked.

"Where?" Josh asked.

"Check this out," Dink said. He held up his right hand. The palm had a black mark on it, like a curvy X. "It's black paint."

"How'd you get that?" Ruth Rose asked.

"I was leaning on that wire fencing," Dink said. "I felt something wet, so I looked at my hand and saw this. I took a closer look at the fencing. Guys, somebody cut a big hole in it!"

"What do you mean?" Ruth Rose asked. "We were standing next to you, and I didn't see any hole in the fencing."

"That's because whoever cut the fencing put it back together again," Dink said. "I think they twisted some wires on to the corners to attach the cutout part, then painted the wires to match the fence," he said. He held out his hand. "That's how I got this."

"Why would anyone cut a hole and patch it up again?" Josh asked.

"I wondered the same thing," Dink said. "Then I figured it out." He walked toward the zoo entrance.

"Do we have to figure it out, too?"

Josh asked, catching up. "Or are you going to tell us?"

Dink stopped walking and looked at his friends. "I don't think Jade climbed a tree and escaped," he said.

"You don't?" asked Ruth Rose.

Dink shook his head. "I think someone cut that hole in the fencing to get inside," he said. "And then they *kidnapped* her!"

CHAPTER FIVE

"Kidnapped!" Josh said. "Who'd steal a leopard?"

"Remember my dad told us people buy leopard fur to make coats?" Dink asked. "Maybe someone—"

"They better not!" Ruth Rose said.

The kids stopped next to the giant lion sculpture. The words SAN DIEGO ZOO were painted in green above the gates.

"How come you didn't tell Dr. Akbar and Debbie about the hole in the fencing?" Ruth Rose asked Dink.

"Because I don't know *who* kidnapped Jade," Dink said. "But I figure it had to be someone who could get into the zoo and into Jade's enclosure at night."

"Dr. Akbar said there are night guards walking around," Josh said. "Wouldn't they notice the kidnappers? It would take time to cut a hole in the fencing, sneak Jade out, and patch up the fence again."

"The guards check out the whole zoo," Dink said. "That means they wouldn't be able to watch Jade's enclosure every minute. The kidnappers would have waited till the guards passed, then cut the hole."

"Okay, but how would they actually *take* Jade?" Josh asked. "She has big teeth and sharp claws!"

Dink started walking toward the gates. "Come on, let's go find out how."

"Back inside?" Josh asked. "How will we get in?"

Dink grinned. "Leopards aren't the only ones who know how to climb," he said.

When they reached the main gates, it

took Dink only nine seconds to leap over.
Josh and Ruth Rose followed him. Two
minutes later, they walked past other
animal enclosures. A hippo rose from a
muddy pond and opened its huge mouth
for a yawn. A flock of bright-pink fla-
mingos fluttered their wings and made
squawking noises.

Dink stopped outside Jade's enclosure. "See?" he said, pointing to the short
wires that had been twisted to hold the
piece of fencing in place. "These little
wires were probably silver-colored, so
they painted them black."

"That's a big hole," Josh said. "A leopard could fit through easy."

"We can fit, too," Dink said. "Ruth
Rose, do you have your pocketknife?"

Ruth Rose found the red Swiss Army
knife in her backpack and opened it, dis-
playing all the tools. "How about this little screwdriver?" she asked.

"Try it," Dink said.

Ruth Rose used the screwdriver to pop off the wires on the four corners. Dink and Josh pulled the section of fencing away. The hole was about five feet tall by three feet wide.

"This is what the kidnappers did last night," Dink said.

Josh peered through the opening. "Are we absolutely, one hundred percent, sure Jade isn't still in there?" he whispered. "Hiding in her cave?"

"I'll find out," Ruth Rose said. She climbed through the hole in the fence and marched toward Jade's cave under the boulders.

Dink poked Josh until he followed Ruth Rose. When Dink climbed through the opening, he looked at the fence wires that had been cut. Near the ground, he spotted something gold-colored stuck on one wire. "Oh no!" he yelled.

CHAPTER SIX

Josh and Ruth Rose came back to the opening in the fence.

Dink showed them what he held in his fingers. "A chunk of Jade's fur!" he said. "It was caught on one of the cut wires!"

"If somebody dragged Jade out—" Josh started to say.

"Nobody could drag her out," Ruth Rose said. "She'd fight like a tiger! Or a leopard."

"Unless they gave her something to make her sleep," Josh said with a sneaky look.

"How?" Ruth Rose asked.

"If I were doing it, I'd put sleeping pills or something in her food," Josh said. "And I'd do it at night, while the guards were in another part of the zoo."

"Wait, could the *guards* be the kidnappers?" Ruth Rose asked. "*They* could have drugged Jade and snatched her last night."

"They'd be pretty silly to do that," Josh said. "The guards are the first ones the cops would go to because they're here at night and they have keys. Besides, they don't feed the animals."

Dink stared at Josh. "You're right," he whispered. "But Dr. Akbar does. We saw him feed Jade those meatballs just before she went into her cave last night. Maybe there was something else in the meatballs! Something other than vitamins."

"You think Dr. Akbar kidnapped Jade?" Ruth Rose asked.

"It would be easy for him," Dink said.

"Nobody would wonder why he was here at night. He has keys to the outside gates. And he could have drugged those meatballs!"

"Well, I think you're wrong!" Ruth Rose said. "He loves Jade. We saw how upset he was when he found out she was gone. He'd never do anything to harm her!"

Dink looked at Ruth Rose. "Then who?" he asked.

"I don't know," Ruth Rose said.

"Let's keep looking," Josh said. "In the movies, one of the bad guys always drops his cell phone or wallet at the scene of the crime."

Dink walked around the little pond.

Ruth Rose crawled into Jade's cave. She backed out holding a bone with teeth marks all over it. "There are a lot of bones in the cave," she said. "Maybe the kidnappers used a bone to drug her."

"Hey, guys, check this out," Dink

said. He was standing next to the pond where the ground was wet. "Someone wearing big shoes or boots was in here!"

Ruth Rose pointed at something else. "Watch out for the leopard poop," she said.

"Animal poop is called *scat*," Josh said. "Don't step in that scat, Pat!"

Dink knelt down to study the footprints. "These might be from the kidnappers," he said.

"Or one of Jade's keepers," Ruth Rose said.

Dink took a picture of the prints with his phone.

The kids left Jade's enclosure through the hole in the fence. Dink and Josh held the cut section in place while Ruth Rose twisted the four wires. Dink snapped a picture.

They walked to a water fountain and took sips. "How much do you think Jade weighs?" Dink asked.

Josh shrugged. "More than we do," he said. "Why?"

"Sixty to one hundred pounds," Ruth Rose said. "I read it on the plaque."

"So she'd be too heavy for one person to carry all the way to the main gates," Dink said. "It's like a half mile down this path. The kidnappers couldn't drive a car or truck through the gates, so how'd they do it?"

"Easy, use one of those cart things," Josh said. "Like the Bug."

"Yeah," Dink said. "And some guy in a uniform dropped Dr. Akbar off in one yesterday. If the carts belong to the

zoo, maybe that guy knows if anyone borrowed one last night."

"Dr. Akbar called him Rob," Ruth Rose said. "And Dr. Akbar said he'd bring the cart back to the maintenance shed."

The kids walked along the path until it joined two other paths. There was a post with directions painted on a wooden sign. An arrow pointed one way for LEOPARD, HIPPO, PRIMATE HOUSE. Another arrow pointed toward REST-ROOMS. A third arrow pointed toward MAINTENANCE.

"Aha!" Josh said.

They hiked a few hundred yards. Jungle foliage lined the path. Strange animal noises came from behind walls and fences.

A wide dirt path led off to the right. At the end of the path stood a small building. A black pickup truck was behind it, and a golf cart was parked near the door. "There it is," Josh said.

As the kids walked down the path, Rob came out of the building. They watched him fill a pail with water from a spigot. Then he picked up a hose and began spraying the cart.

CHAPTER SEVEN

"Oh no!" Dink muttered. "That's Rob, and he's washing away the clues!"

"What clues?" Josh asked.

"If the kidnappers put Jade in that cart, some of her fur might have rubbed off," Dink said. "We'll never find it now!"

"Oh yeah?" Ruth Rose said. She sprinted down the path, waving her hands. She reached Rob and started talking to him. He stopped what he was doing and looked at Ruth Rose.

"What's she up to?" Josh whispered.

Dink grinned. "Saving the clues," he said. "Come on!"

The boys ran down the path just as Ruth Rose said, "A leopard escaped! It could be anywhere!" She waved her arms at the trees surrounding the building.

"Jade got loose?" Rob asked.

"Yes!" Ruth Rose said. "And she might be dangerous!"

"Wow," the man said. "Thanks for telling me!"

Dink was standing behind the cart. He saw a piece of golden fuzz stuck on the backseat. While Rob was shutting off the water, Dink grabbed the fur and slipped it into his pocket.

"Is this your golf cart?" Ruth Rose asked Rob.

"Naw, it belongs to the zoo," he said, tapping the pocket of his uniform shirt where it said ROB WOLFF, MAINTENANCE. "We have a bunch of these carts, and I take care of them and the Bug that the TV people are using. I fix them if they

break down, plus anything else that goes wrong around here."

"Aren't you worried someone might steal them?" Ruth Rose asked. "I mean if they're just parked here at night?"

Rob shook his head. "Only folks who work here full-time can use them," he said. "I have a set of keys, and so do Dr. Akbar, the head zookeeper, and the guards. Dr. Fern, the zoo director, also has keys. At night, the carts are sitting right here. I keep the keys inside."

While Rob was talking to Ruth Rose, Dink looked around. A picnic table sat on the lawn near the pickup truck. In the truck's bed, bales of hay were stacked next to a sack with the words LLAMA PELLETS printed on the side. A blue tarp covered a bunch of tools.

A bumper sticker had LLAMA LOVE printed over a llama's face. Dink took a picture.

"I'd better finish washing this thing," Rob said, nodding toward the cart. "So if . . ."

"We have to take off anyway," Dink said. "My dad will get worried. He's expecting us."

Dink started back along the path, with Josh and Ruth Rose right behind him.

"My dad's expecting us?" Josh said. "He's not expecting us till noon."

"I know," Dink said.

"I saw you take something out of the cart's backseat," Ruth Rose said.

"More Jade fur," Dink said. "Good thing you stopped him before he washed it away!"

"That doesn't mean *Jade* was on the seat," Josh said. "Anyone who *touched* Jade could have left that fur. Dr. Akbar probably has some of Jade's fur on his pants. It could just rub off on the seat."

"You're right," Dink said. "There are too many people who go in Jade's enclosure and drive around in those carts."

"But only one of them kidnapped her!" Ruth Rose said. "Or two, I guess."

"Unless the kidnapper really *is* Dr. Akbar," Josh said. "And he was just faking being all upset."

"He had tears in his eyes," Ruth Rose said. "Kidnappers don't usually cry!"

"If the kidnapper really did drug Jade's food, maybe we should find out who's in charge of feeding her," Dink said.

"Right," Ruth Rose said. "There are thousands of animals in the zoo. Where does their food come from?"

"No prob, Bob," Josh said. "Get the zoo website on your phone. There's probably a map of this whole place."

The kids sat on a bench, with Dink in the middle. He found the San Diego Zoo website and clicked on its home page. "Here's the map," he said.

The map showed the paths, enclosures, and buildings on the zoo grounds. The buildings had tiny numbers next to them. A list on the bottom of the map named each building.

Dink enlarged the map. "Here it is, a kitchen!" he said. He turned his phone sideways, enlarging the map again. "It's down the path we're on, and around a corner."

The kids headed down the path. They came to the reptile house, a giant stone building. "Want to go in and say hi to your friends?" Dink asked Josh.

"So. Not. Funny," Josh said.

The path bent left around a small pond, and the kids saw a big wooden structure standing in a grove of trees. It looked like it was once a home, with a wide porch across the front. A woman in a white uniform sat on the steps, drinking a soda.

"Now what?" Ruth Rose muttered.

"I've got this one," Josh said. He marched up to the porch, stopping a few feet from the woman. "Excuse me, but we're looking for the place that makes food for the animals."

"You found it," the woman said. "This is the kitchen."

"Great!" Josh said. "See, we're here with Parker Stone and the *Roger to the Rescue* film crew, but I really want to be a zookeeper someday. It would be awesome if I could interview you!"

Dink and Ruth Rose stood a few yards away. "Josh wants to work in a zoo?" Dink whispered.

"You should talk to my boss, Sofi," the woman said. "She's inside."

Josh smiled. "Do you think she'd let three kids interview her?" he asked. "We came all the way from Connecticut!"

"Oh brother," Ruth Rose said.

The woman stood up. "I'll ask her," she said. "What's your name, hon?"

"Josh Pinto," Josh said. "My friends are Dink and Ruth Rose. They're really into animals, too."

Ruth Rose giggled.

The woman walked inside. Josh turned and grinned like a monkey at Dink and Ruth Rose. "Come on!" he whispered.

CHAPTER EIGHT

Dink and Ruth Rose ran up to the porch. A minute later, the woman appeared in the doorway. "Come in," she said.

The kids followed her into a huge kitchen. Everything was white and shiny, like on a TV cooking show. About ten other people were in the room, all wearing latex gloves, white uniforms, and paper caps. They were chopping meat, vegetables, and fruit at long stainless steel counters.

Plastic bins were lined up on the counters. Each bin cover was labeled with a different animal name. Dink watched one worker take a package the size of a football from a refrigerator. It was wrapped in brown paper. When he peeled off the paper, a pile of bloody bones fell onto the counter. The guy weighed the bones, then tossed them into the bin with TIGER on the cover.

Dink took more pictures.

"That's Sofi," the woman said, pointing to a tall woman making notes on a whiteboard with a marker. "Go on over and say hi."

The three kids walked through the kitchen, passing a row of refrigerators. When one of the workers opened a fridge door, Dink saw trays of meat and bones. He took more pictures, but he didn't like the smell.

The woman turned when the kids reached her. "I'm Sofi French," she said. "And you are . . . ?"

"I'm Josh Pinto," Josh said. "These are my friends Dink and Ruth Rose."

The woman nodded. "Let's go into my office."

They followed her to a door that said S. FRENCH, DIETITIAN. Sofi sat at a desk and motioned the kids toward some chairs. "Okay, talk to me," she said. "I've got ten minutes."

"Do you mind if my friend gets a video of this?" Josh asked, pointing to Dink. "He wants to be a movie director when he grows up!"

I do? thought Dink.

Sofi French shrugged. "No problem," she said.

Dink tapped the video icon on his phone. "Okay," he said.

Sofi pulled her own phone from a pocket and set it on her desk. "Shoot," she said, smiling at the kids.

"Um, we were wondering who feeds the animals," Dink said.

"Zoo staff does that every morning," Sofi said. "Sometimes the keepers use

food treats to help with the training, like rewarding your dog with a cookie. Some of my kitchen interns also like to help with the feeding. I don't, because I'm allergic to animal fur."

Sofi's phone pinged. She glanced at it, then tapped the screen like she was checking texts or emails.

"Dr. Akbar gave Jade some meatballs last night," Ruth Rose said.

At the word *meatballs,* Sofi looked up from her phone. She stared at Ruth Rose, then looked over Ruth Rose's shoulder. Dink saw a bulletin board on the wall.

"Yes, Dr. Akbar picks up a few baggies of meatballs here every day," Sofi said. "I know he gives them to Jade as a treat."

Dink thought Sofi looked nervous. Her eyes were blinking rapidly and kept going back to the bulletin board.

"Did you know that Jade escaped from her enclosure?" he asked.

"Yes, of course, we all know," Sofi

said. "There's a huge search going on."
She stood. "I have to get back to work.
Can we wrap this up?"

"If an animal gets sick, can you put
their medicine inside a meatball?" Dink
asked.

"Yes, or in with their regular food,"
Sofi said.

"I saw a TV show where this tiger
had a broken paw," Josh said. "They had
to make the tiger sleep while they fixed
it. Do you do that here in the zoo?"

"Yes, we had a lion with a bad tooth-
ache," Sofi said. "But the animal wouldn't
eat anything, so hiding medicine in the
food didn't work."

"What did you do?" Dink asked.

"Dr. Akbar shot a knockout medicine
into him with a dart gun," Sofi said.

She walked to the door and held it
open. While Josh and Ruth Rose walked
out, Dink took a picture of the bulletin
board.

CHAPTER NINE

The kids left Sofi's office and passed through the kitchen again. Dink noticed a worker slicing meat into chunks, using a long, curved knife. The guy's gloves and apron were covered with blood. Dink felt a shiver on his arms as he hurried after Josh and Ruth Rose.

"So now we know that if someone drugged Jade, they could have done it with a dart gun or a meatball!" Josh said when they were outside.

"Almost anybody could have thrown some drugged food into her enclosure," Ruth Rose said.

"You're right, but who could have cut a hole in the fence and taken her out?" Dink asked.

They walked past the primate house. Monkey screeches came through the barred windows.

Just then, they heard footsteps. "Hey, stop!" a voice called out.

They turned around to see Dr. Akbar jogging toward them. "What're you doing here?" he asked. "I thought you kids left the zoo grounds."

"Josh wanted to visit the kitchen," Ruth Rose blurted out. "He has to do a report when we get back home, and he—"

"Okay, but you have to leave the zoo right now," Dr. Akbar interrupted. "This whole place is a crime scene!"

"What crime?" Dink asked. But he already knew.

Dr. Akbar wiped sweat from his face. "Jade didn't escape. Someone took her!" he said. "We found a hole cut in the

fence. The zoo director got a ransom text ten minutes ago. The kidnappers want the zoo to pay to get Jade back!"

The three kids stared at Dr. Akbar. Dink decided not to tell him they already knew about the hole.

"Come on, I'll walk you to the gates," Dr. Akbar said.

"How much money did the kidnappers ask for?" Josh asked as they hiked along the path.

"The zoo director doesn't want the amount known," Dr. Akbar said. "But I know it's more than a million dollars. The text said the kidnappers want the money by three o'clock. The zoo doesn't have that kind of cash, so Dr. Fern is working with our bank."

"Three o'clock today?" Josh squawked.

Dr. Akbar nodded and looked at his watch. "The kidnappers told us to put the money in a suitcase and leave it at a closed-up gas station called Flip's," he said. "If they don't find it there, they said we'd never get Jade back!"

Dr. Akbar checked his watch again, then hurried up the path. The kids ran after him.

When they reached the exit, they saw a police van parked outside the gates. Two officers in uniform got out when they saw Dr. Akbar.

"Kids, I'm sorry about this," Dr. Akbar told them. "I feel awful about the TV show, too. We were all looking forward to having Parker share the Amur story with his viewers. If we get Jade back, maybe . . ."

Dr. Akbar shook his head. He let the kids out through the gates, and the police officers came in.

The kids hiked across the parking lot. When they passed the three trailers, Josh said, "Wait till Parker, Debbie, and Sparky find out someone stole Jade! They were already bummed when they thought she escaped."

Ruth Rose stared at the three trailers. "Guys, what if *they* kidnapped her?" she asked quietly.

"*Who?*" Dink said.

Ruth Rose pointed at the trailers. "What if it was Debbie and Sparky?" she whispered.

"Why would *they* kidnap her?" Josh asked. "With Jade gone, they don't have a TV show."

"I think you're wrong," Ruth Rose said. "If Jade got kidnapped, their show would be even better!"

"What do you mean?" Dink asked.

"Okay, suppose Debbie or Sparky came up with a plan to kidnap Jade," Ruth Rose said. "They make a big deal out of the kidnapping. Then somehow Parker *finds* Jade, gets her away from the kidnappers, and brings her back to the zoo. They do a *Roger to the Rescue* show about how Roger rescues a pregnant endangered leopard!"

"That would explain why Debbie wanted pictures of the empty cave and enclosure," Josh said. "They'll use it as part of the show!"

"So you think Debbie or Sparky sent the ransom text?" Dink asked.

"That would work!" Josh said. "After they collect the ransom money, Parker just happens to discover where Jade is, and he rescues her. Those three get to keep the money, and the zoo gets Jade back!"

CHAPTER TEN

The kids walked past the trailers to the road that led into Balboa Park. "I don't know, guys," Dink said. "I can't see Parker as a kidnapper. Remember, *he* got kidnapped last year in Arizona."

"Maybe Debbie and Sparky planned the kidnapping but only told Parker after Jade disappeared. They'd have to let him in on it so he could rescue Jade," Josh said. "She could be stashed in one of their trailers!"

Dink laughed. "They'd have to be pretty bold to hide Jade on zoo property," he said.

"I agree," Ruth Rose said. "Besides, Parker is too nice to go along with that plan. His TV show is all about *helping* animals."

Suddenly something flew over their heads. It made a whirring noise.

"It's that drone again!" Ruth Rose said.

The white object buzzed over some trees on the right side of the road, then disappeared.

"Let's see where it went!" Josh said. "Maybe it's delivering ice cream to someone!" He started running up the road.

Dink and Ruth Rose jogged after Josh. They found him on the other side of the trees. "It went behind that building," Josh said. They were across the road from the old house they'd seen last night.

"It doesn't look so creepy in daylight," Ruth Rose said.

"Yeah, it does," Josh said. "Probably filled with ghosts and spiders."

"Two of your favorite things," Dink teased.

"Yuck, Chuck," Josh said.

They crossed the road and followed a weedy gravel driveway. When they reached the house, they stopped and gawked.

The house's green paint was peeling off.

Two of the porch steps were missing.

A small tree grew through the rotting porch floor.

The front door and windows were covered with plywood.

"I hear ghosts," Josh whispered.

"Ghosts don't make noise," Ruth Rose said. She dropped her backpack to the ground.

Dink checked out the yard, which was more like an overgrown field than a lawn. It was mostly bushes with thorny branches and brown grass. "I don't see the drone," he said.

"Maybe it didn't land here," Josh said. "It just looked like it was zooming right over this place."

"Let's check around back," Ruth Rose said.

Behind the house, the yard was more dead grass and wild bushes. The kids stepped over a rotting wooden fence as they walked around the building.

Every window was boarded up. The back door was also covered with plywood.

Small cellar windows close to the ground were caked with dirt and cobwebs. "That's how the ghosts get in and out," Josh said, pointing at one of the windows.

"Or there," Dink said. He pointed to a metal door that seemed to lead to the cellar. A padlocked chain was looped through the door handle.

They saw a small air conditioner in a window, dripping water from one corner.

"I wonder how long this place has been empty," Ruth Rose said.

"Debbie said a long time," Dink said. "Anyway, I don't see the drone."

"Let's get back to the Zoo-Tel," Josh said. "There's a pistachio cone and a swimming pool in my future!"

"What, you don't want to go inside this house?" Ruth Rose asked. "Maybe the ghosts left you some ice cream in the freezer!"

"Not happening," Josh said. He marched toward the road, waving fingers over his shoulder.

Dink and Ruth Rose followed him. "I agree with Josh about a swim," Ruth Rose said, grabbing her backpack.

Suddenly Dink stopped. "Wait," he said. He looked at the house. "Why is it dripping?"

He jogged back around the house and stopped next to the window holding the air conditioner. Josh and Ruth Rose followed him.

"See, water is leaking out," Dink said. He knelt and put his hand on the ground under the air conditioner. "The dirt is damp down here."

"So what?" Josh said. "Our air conditioner at home is always dripping."

"Ours, too," Ruth Rose said. "It's condensation."

"But air conditioners don't do that unless they've been used recently," Dink said.

He looked at Josh and Ruth Rose with raised eyebrows. "If this house is abandoned," he whispered, "who turned on the air conditioner?"

CHAPTER ELEVEN

Dink placed his hand on the air conditioner's casing. "This thing isn't that old," he said. "And I can feel the motor."

"Zombies like it cool!" Josh moaned. "Let's get out of here before one comes out and cuts our heads off!"

"No one's in this house, Josh. It's all boarded up," Ruth Rose said. "Maybe the owners left the air conditioner on for some reason."

Dink walked up to the back door and tugged on the plywood covering it. "No one opens *this* door," he said. "Not even a zombie, Josh."

They returned to the front of the house, checking more windows. All had plywood nailed in place. The wood was stained, like it had been there for a long time.

"Can we leave, Steve?" Josh asked. "This house is old and nasty."

Dink climbed onto the porch, being careful not to step where the wood had rotted. He tugged on the plywood over the door and windows. "This wood is real old," he said. "The nails and screws are rusty."

Ruth Rose looked at the plywood behind Dink. "But . . . *everything* should be rusty," she muttered, then ran around the side of the house.

Dink and Josh trotted after her. She stopped at the metal door that covered the cellar steps.

Ruth Rose pointed to the padlock. "That padlock is shiny," she said. "Like someone just bought it."

"You're right," Dink said. "The chain looks new, too." He leaned over and yanked on the lock, but it stayed shut.

Suddenly Dink jumped back.

"Spider bite you?" Josh teased.

"No, I heard a noise down there," Dink said.

"What kind of noise?" Josh asked. "Like a zombie?"

"I don't know," Dink whispered.

Dink grabbed the chain and pulled, making it clang against the metal. "I heard it again!"

Ruth Rose put her ear next to the metal door. She yanked the chain, and then *she* jumped back. "Wow, I heard it, too!" she said. "It sounded like coughing."

"You guys are so lame," Josh scoffed. "You're trying to scare me. I don't really believe in zombies, you know."

"We're not joking," Dink said. "Put your ear there."

Josh rolled his eyes, but he got on his

knees and leaned his head near the metal
door. Dink tugged the chain, knocking it
against the door.

Josh grinned. "Nothing! See, I told—"

Suddenly Josh leaped away from the
door, bumping into Dink. "Something
growled!" he yelped.

"Maybe someone's dog got trapped!"
Ruth Rose said. "Can we bust this lock?"

"Um, we can't just break into someone's house," Dink said.

"Then we should call the police!"
Ruth Rose insisted. "They rescue cats
and dogs all the time."

Just then, they heard a voice behind
them: "Yo, what's going on?"

They turned around to see a guy
walking his bike around the corner of
the house. He was holding a small drone.

Dink thought the man's face looked
familiar, and he didn't like the look in
his eyes.

"Who're you guys?" the man asked.

He leaned his bike against the house. Dink noticed a package in the basket.

"We were hiking and thought we heard a dog barking," Ruth Rose said. "It sounded like it was coming from down there." She pointed to the locked cellar stairs.

The man stared at her. "Yeah, that's . . . Zoomer, my sister's dog," he said. "She bought this place from the zoo and lets me crash here. Zoomer stays with me so he won't have to be alone at my sister's apartment."

Dink remembered where he'd seen this guy's face: on Sofi's bulletin board. "Is your sister Sofi French?" he asked.

"Yeah, I'm her brother Lester," the man said. "How do you know my sister?"

"Um, we met her at the zoo," Dink said. "We went to the kitchen because my friends and I want to be zookeepers and learn how to feed the animals."

Dink felt himself blush at the lie he'd just told.

"Is that a drone?" Josh asked.

Lester held out the contraption. "Yeah, I like to fly it where there's no traffic," he said. "I can usually get it to come back here, but this time something went wrong. I had to go look for it."

A phone dinged, and Dink reached for his. But he had no incoming text. Lester pulled his phone from a pocket and glanced at the screen. Then he looked at the kids. "Do you live around here?" he asked. He wasn't smiling anymore.

"We're on vacation from Connecticut," Dink said. "With my dad." He glanced at Josh and Ruth Rose. "We'd better get going, guys."

Lester watched them walk away.

As soon as they were out of sight, Dink got on his cell phone. He opened his photos and scrolled. "Here, take a look at this," he said, showing them Lester's picture on Sofi's bulletin board in the zoo kitchen.

"I think he's lying about babysitting Sofi's dog in that house," Dink said. He looked at Josh and Ruth Rose. "Remember Sofi told us she's allergic to furry animals? Then why would she own a dog?"

"So that wasn't a dog named Zoomer we heard?" Josh said.

Dink shook his head. "Nope, I think Lester just made up a name," he said. "A decal on the side of his drone spells out Zoomer. That's the *drone's* name, and it's probably the first thing he could think of as a name for the *dog.*"

"The dog that isn't there," Josh said.

"Let's keep walking," Ruth Rose said. "He might be watching us."

They walked to the road and stopped behind some thick bushes.

"Okay, so why did Sofi's brother tell us he's babysitting her dog if she doesn't have a dog?" Josh asked.

Dink stared back at the house. "Because he didn't want us to figure out what's *really* making those noises," he said quietly.

Josh looked at Dink with eyes the size of doughnuts. "What *is* making the noises?" he croaked.

"Jade," Dink said.

CHAPTER TWELVE

"WHAT?" Ruth Rose and Josh cried.

Dink put his finger to his lips. "Not so loud," he said.

"Dude, you think that was *Jade* we just heard?" Josh asked.

Dink nodded. "When we were in the zoo kitchen, we saw them chopping up meat for the animals, right?" he said. "The meat was wrapped in brown paper. This guy had a package in his bike basket wrapped in the same kind of paper. I don't think Lester was chasing his drone. I think he was bringing food for Jade!"

"Oh my gosh!" Ruth Rose said.

"I was inches away from a hungry leopard!" Josh said.

"This house is a perfect place to keep Jade until he gets the ransom money," Dink continued. "The house looks abandoned, so no one ever comes near it."

"We have to go tell Dr. Akbar!" Ruth Rose said.

The kids raced back toward the zoo as fast as they could run. When they reached the parking lot, they were out of breath and sweating. Parker was sitting outside his trailer, working on his laptop.

"Guys, what's up with the running?" he asked.

"I think we just found Jade!" Dink said.

"Jade?" Parker said. "Who . . . oh, the missing leopard. You found her?"

"The guy who kidnapped her is keeping her in an old house!" Ruth Rose said.

"Whoa. *Kidnapped?*" Parker said. "I thought the doc told us she jumped over the fence or something."

"No! Someone cut through it and took her!" Dink said. He showed Parker the picture on his phone. "They put the fence piece back in so no one would notice the hole."

Parker shut his laptop. "Wait till Debbie hears about this!" he said.

Dink looked at the Bug, which was parked outside Debbie's trailer. "Where is she?"

Parker grinned. "I think she and Sparky like each other," he said. "They went for a walk a little while ago."

"Can you really drive the Bug?" Dink asked.

"No problem," Parker said. "I drive my dad's golf cart, and it's a lot more complicated."

"Then drive us to find Dr. Akbar!"

They piled into the Bug, and Parker started it up. He zoomed across the parking lot, then stopped. "Oops, forgot something," he said, and turned the Bug around.

Leaving the cart running, he dashed into his trailer and came back holding a plastic card. "This gets us through the gates," he said.

Parker passed the police van and pulled up to the farthest gate on the right. He inserted the card into a slot. The gate opened, and the Bug shot through.

"How do we find Dr. Akbar?" he asked Dink, who was sitting in the front passenger seat. "This place has a zillion paths."

"Go to Jade's enclosure," Ruth Rose said.

"The scene of the crime!" Josh yelled from the backseat.

Parker turned the Bug to the right and headed down the path. They passed lions and tigers and giraffes, all behind enclosure walls and fences.

"There they are!" Dink said.

Dr. Akbar and the two police officers were standing outside Jade's enclosure.

When Parker stopped the Bug, Dr. Akbar shook his head and walked over. "I thought I asked you—"

"We found Jade!" Ruth Rose cried.

Dr. Akbar looked at Parker, who shrugged. "That's what they told me," he said. "I'm just the driver here."

"We think the kidnapper is keeping her in an old house down the road," Dink explained.

"It's a zombie house!" Josh added.

"You said *we think*," Dr. Akbar said. "Did you actually *see* Jade?"

"We heard her with our own eyes!" Josh said.

Dr. Akbar raised his eyebrows. "How . . ."

"We heard funny noises from inside the cellar, like the ones Jade makes," Dink explained.

"What kind of noises?"

"Coughing and growling," Ruth Rose said.

"Jade sometimes does that," Dr. Akbar said. "It's her way of talking."

"Sounds like people noises," one of the officers said. DIGGS, W. was printed on a tag pinned to his shirt.

Dr. Akbar introduced the two officers to Parker and the three kids.

"What else did you see . . . or hear?" the other officer asked. Her name tag said BROWN, F.

"After we heard the noises, a guy

showed up," Dink went on. "We think he's the kidnapper! He said we heard a dog, but we think . . . I know he was lying. And he had a package of something wrapped in brown paper. Like the paper they use in the zoo kitchen. I think it was meat for Jade!"

"Tell us about this guy," Officer Diggs said.

"His sister Sofi works in the zoo," Ruth Rose said.

"I know Sofi," Dr. Akbar said. "You really think this kidnapper is her brother?"

Dink nodded. "He said he's Sofi's brother and his name is Lester."

"Has the zoo paid the ransom money yet?" Officer Brown asked Dr. Akbar.

"Not yet," he said. "But the bank is dropping it off at Dr. Fern's office anytime now."

"Then we'd better stop them," Officer Brown said.

CHAPTER THIRTEEN

Dr. Akbar took out his phone and chose a number on speed dial. "Um, Dr. Fern, this is David Akbar. Don't take the money to Flip's! I have reason to believe Jade is nearby and safe," he said. "Some children and that boy who's doing the TV show say they found her. Right, I will."

Dr. Akbar hung up. "Officers, can you take us to the house?" he asked.

"Where is it?" Officer Diggs asked.

"Down the road," Ruth Rose said. "We can show you!"

"I don't think anyone lives there," Dink said. "It's all boarded up."

"Probably filled with ghosts," Josh muttered.

"I think I know that place," Officer Brown said. "I grew up around here. My brothers and I rode our bikes up and down this road all the time."

"Dr. Akbar," Officer Diggs put in, "how do you know that the people who texted the ransom note really have your leopard? They could be scamming you for the money."

"I asked for proof," he said.

He opened to his recent texts and showed them a video. Everyone leaned close to look. It was Jade's face. Her eyes were closed.

The video moved, showing a blue tarp wrapped around her body, held in place with ropes. The tarp was resting on a layer of straw. The video moved again, showing Jade's long tail, slowly swishing against the floor.

"You're sure that's the right leopard?"

Officer Diggs asked. "Don't they all look alike?"

Dr. Akbar pointed to Jade's left ear. "She has a nick right there," he said. "That's Jade. And her whiskers and tail are moving, so she's alive!"

Everyone jumped into the Bug. Parker drove, with Dr. Akbar in the front passenger seat. He kept his black doctor bag on his lap. The three kids sat behind them. Officers Diggs and Brown were in the back, hanging on as Parker headed along the path.

When they got to the gates, Dr. Akbar used his pass and they went through. On the other side, Parker pulled the Bug next to the police van.

"I call dibs on shotgun!" Josh said.

"Sorry, buddy," Officer Diggs said. "I have dibs on shotgun, and you sit in the back with your pals!"

The kids piled into the back, with Dr. Akbar and Parker in front of them.

"Please buckle up, everyone," Officer Brown said.

The van sped across the parking lot, past the trailers, and onto the road through Balboa Park.

"Right there," Josh said a minute later, pointing at the old house.

Officer Diggs pulled a few yards into the gravel driveway. He stopped the van under overhanging tree branches, where it wouldn't be seen. The abandoned house stood a hundred feet in front of them.

"Jade is being kept there?" Dr. Akbar asked. "And Sofi's brother is with her?"

Dink nodded. "There's a door to a cellar around back, and that's where we heard the noises," he said.

"How do you want to run this, Flo?" Officer Diggs asked Officer Brown.

"We park here and go in on foot," Officer Brown said. "You take the front, and I'll go around back. The windows are covered, so he probably won't see us coming. Civilians stay in the van."

"We have to stay here?" Josh asked.

Officer Brown turned and looked at the three kids and Parker. "Absolutely," she said. "We're dealing with a kidnapper who might be dangerous. And a wild animal! I need you kids to stay put."

Officer Diggs looked at Dr. Akbar. "How dangerous is this leopard?" he asked.

"If I'm with you, Jade should be fine," he answered. "I brought something to keep her calm."

"Like what?" Officer Diggs asked.

Dr. Akbar held up a baggie. "Meatballs," he said. "Her favorite, but these will make her groggy."

"Then you come with us," Officer Diggs said.

"My pleasure," Dr. Akbar said. He winked at Josh.

"There's a big padlock on the cellar door," Ruth Rose told the officers. "It was locked."

Officer Brown nodded. "Thanks," she said. She pulled a bolt cutter from under her seat. "This is *my* key."

The two officers and Dr. Akbar stepped out onto the weedy driveway

and began walking toward the house. Dr. Akbar had his doctor bag, and Officer Brown carried the bolt cutter.

Officer Diggs turned around and jogged back to the front passenger-side window. He reached in, opened the glove compartment, and pulled out a bag of M&M's.

"Don't tell Officer Brown I'm giving you her goodies," he said, dropping the candy on Parker's lap. "And don't touch any buttons or knobs."

Officer Diggs trotted after his partner and Dr. Akbar.

"I still don't think it's fair that we have to stay in this van," Josh said.

Parker stretched his legs out. "I agree. This is bogus," he said. "They treat us like kids."

"We are kids," Dink reminded him.

"You're kids," Parker said. "I'm a teenager."

"I need a bathroom," Josh announced.

Everyone looked at him.

"You're kidding, right?" Dink asked.

Josh shook his head. "I need to go, Mo."

Parker laughed. "Just go behind a bush," he said. "Like the bears."

Josh climbed out of the van and walked toward some bushes. In a minute, he was out of sight.

The others waited in the silent van.

Dr. Akbar and the two officers didn't return.

Josh didn't return.

Dink checked his watch. "How long—"

"Oh no!" Ruth Rose said. She pointed out the window.

Josh was on the driveway. But he wasn't heading toward the police van. He was running *away* from it.

"Where's he going?" Parker asked, sitting up.

"Where do you *think* he's going?" Dink asked. "To see Jade get rescued!"

CHAPTER FOURTEEN

"Then I'm going, too!" Parker cried. He opened the side door and stepped out. "You guys coming?"

"Officer Brown told us to stay put," Dink said. "Maybe we should—"

"Come on, Dink," Ruth Rose said. "What if Josh gets in trouble? He needs us!" She joined Parker.

"Now we're talking!" Parker said. "Josh needs us!"

Dink shook his head. *Josh is running toward a kidnapper and a leopard. What could possibly go wrong?* he thought as he hopped out of the van.

Parker, Dink, and Ruth Rose crept up the driveway, trying not to step on fallen branches or into potholes. Dink looked toward the house but didn't see anyone.

They stopped in front of the rotting porch. Parker shook his head. "My dad's in construction," he said. "He'd tear this place down in a minute."

Except for birds, Dink didn't hear a sound. "Where is everyone?" he whispered. "No one's here."

"Josh would say the zombies ate them," Ruth Rose whispered back. "But they're probably behind the house."

"What're we waiting for?" Parker asked.

Dink and Ruth Rose followed him around the side of the house.

The padlock and chain were on the ground. The metal door was open. Dusty concrete steps led into the dark cellar.

Ruth Rose stood on the top step, looking down. "Is anybody there?" she asked.

Dink and Parker stood behind her, looking over her shoulder.

Dr. Akbar appeared at the bottom of the steps. "You kids are never where you're supposed to be," he said.

"We're looking for our friend Josh," Ruth Rose said. "He left the van, and we can't find him!"

Officer Brown came and stood next to Dr. Akbar. "If Josh is the redhead," she said, "he's down here teaching Officer Diggs about leopard poop. You might as well join the party."

Dink, Parker, and Ruth Rose walked down the steps into a room with a dirt floor and low ceiling. It smelled old and wet. With three adults and four kids, the small space was crowded.

"It smells like my cat's litter box," Parker said.

"It's leopard scat," Josh said. "This is where that guy kept Jade!"

As Dink's eyes adjusted to the dark

room, he looked around. The old stone walls were damp. Wooden beams over his head dripped cobwebs. In the middle of the floor, he saw the blue tarp and a pile of rope.

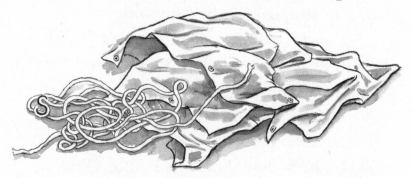

"Jade was definitely kept here," Dr. Akbar said. "This is where the texted video was shot. But they moved her again!"

Officer Diggs kicked at the tarp. "Whoever moved her out of here left this," he said. "Like maybe they were in a hurry."

"Wrapping the tarp around Jade when they took her out of the zoo would make her easier to carry," Dr. Akbar said. "But why didn't they wrap her this time?"

"They must have been in a rush," Officer Brown said.

"Lester French got a text while we were talking to him," Dink said. "Maybe someone told him you guys were coming!"

"He's real skinny and short," Josh said. "I don't think he could move Jade by himself, and he didn't have a car."

"If he got a warning, he had to get the leopard out of here fast," Officer Brown said. "Maybe he called a buddy with a truck."

Dink flashed back to the pickup truck they'd seen at Rob's maintenance shed. In his mind, he saw bales of hay near a blue tarp, like the one here on the floor.

"We know someone who owns a truck," Dink said. He took out his phone and found the pictures he'd been taking all morning. He swiped until he came to Rob Wolff's face on the bulletin board. Then he swiped again, showing the black pickup behind the maintenance shed. He showed the picture to the officers and Dr. Akbar.

"A blue tarp," Officer Brown said.

"Wait, I know that truck," Dr. Akbar said. "It belongs to Rob Wolff, our maintenance guy. How did you get this picture?"

"Um, we met him," Dink said. "This morning."

"You kids seem to meet a lot of people," Officer Diggs said.

"Plenty of folks drive black pickups," Officer Brown said. "And these blue tarps are everywhere. I have one in *my* truck and a couple in my cellar! None of this proves the maintenance guy helped steal the leopard."

"Dr. Akbar, does the zoo have other kinds of leopards?" Ruth Rose asked.

"Yes, we have snow leopards and Asian leopards," he said. "Why?"

"Because when I told Rob Wolff that a leopard had escaped, he said, 'Jade got loose?'" Ruth Rose said. "If the zoo has other leopards, how did he know I was talking about *Jade*?"

CHAPTER FIFTEEN

"Lester and Rob could be in it together," Josh said. "Lester could have used his drone to drop a drugged meatball into Jade's enclosure. Then Rob cut that hole in the fence so he and Lester could drag her out!"

"Meatballs now?" Officer Diggs said. "What meatballs?"

"Sofi told us they give animals medicine in food," Dink explained. "They use meatballs. Maybe her brother stole something to make Jade sleepy and fed it to her inside a meatball."

"The zoo kitchen does keep a small supply of drugs with the vitamins,"

Dr. Akbar said. "I don't know Sofi's brother, but I do know Rob Wolff. I can't believe he'd be involved in this kidnapping scheme."

"Some people do bad things for money," Officer Brown said.

Dr. Akbar shook his head. "Maybe you're right," he muttered.

"How much are we talking about?" Officer Diggs asked him.

"Two million dollars," Dr. Akbar said.

"Cute," Officer Brown said. "They each get a million."

"All right, back in the van, everyone!" Officer Diggs said. "Doc, can you direct us to the zoo maintenance shed?"

"Of course, but if Rob is one of the kidnappers, I doubt he'd bring Jade back to the zoo," Dr. Akbar said.

"Then where would he stash her?" Officer Diggs asked.

Dr. Akbar shrugged. "I have no idea," he said. "But let me try something."

He tapped his phone and called the office at the zoo. "Hi, this is Dr. Akbar again. Can you give me an address for Rob Wolff, the maintenance man? . . . Of course, thank you."

Dr. Akbar held the phone away from his mouth. "They're looking," he said.

"While the bad guy gets away," Officer Brown muttered.

"Oh, thank you," Dr. Akbar said into his phone before putting it in his pocket. "Apparently Rob Wolff put a post office box number as his address."

"Maybe he has a barn or other out-building where he could hide a leopard," Officer Brown said.

"Wait," Dr. Akbar said. "He once asked me for the name of a vet who treats farm animals."

"I saw a bag of llama food in the truck," Dink said. "And he has a llama bumper sticker."

"So maybe he keeps llamas," Officer

Brown said. "If you drive out five or ten miles, some people have horses and chickens on their property. There could be llamas, too, I guess."

"Maybe that vet knows," Ruth Rose said. "If they treat Rob's animals, they would know where Rob lives, wouldn't they?"

"Brilliant!" Officer Diggs said. "Doc, call the guy!"

"*Her* name is Josephine Curtis," Dr. Akbar said as he tapped his phone. "But everyone calls her Jo."

Dr. Akbar finished his call and dropped his phone into a pocket. "Jo Curtis says Rob has a few llamas and chickens."

"Did she tell you where he lives?" Officer Brown asked.

"Drive eight miles south on this road," Dr. Akbar said. "Look for a mailbox on the right, next to a dirt driveway. There will be a wolf's head painted on the mailbox. His place is up that dirt drive."

"Are we going to arrest him?" Parker asked.

"We need to find Jade!" Dr. Akbar said. "She could have her baby leopard at any time!"

"First things first," Officer Brown said. "We're going to look for this leopard. As for Rob, all we know for sure is that he had a blue tarp in his truck. And some hay. Can't arrest a man for that."

"But he knows Sofi's brother," Josh said. "And he knew Jade was missing before anyone else. We should arrest them both!"

Officer Diggs grinned at Josh. "Good thing you're not a cop," he said. "What we'll do is show up at his place and have a chat. See what he says."

"Great plan," Officer Brown said.

"Let's boogie!" Parker said.

"We're going to boogie you all back to the zoo first," Officer Diggs said. "Officer Brown and I will take it from here."

"But why?" Josh asked. "We found Jade!"

"And we're grateful," Officer Diggs said. "But we don't take kids on operations. We have a kidnapper and a wild animal to deal with. I want you safe back at the zoo."

"But I have to go with you," Dr. Akbar said. "If we do find Jade, she might need me. And if you're with me, she won't try to attack you!"

Officer Diggs sighed. "Okay. Get in the van, everyone," he said.

Soon the kids and Parker were standing by the lion sculpture in front of the zoo gates. They watched the police van zoom out to the road and disappear.

"So not fair," Parker said. "I want to be there when they catch this guy."

"But Officers Diggs and Brown are right," Dink said. "They can't bring us with them."

"So now what do we do?" Josh asked.

"I guess I'll call my dad to come and get us," Dink said.

Just then, Debbie and Sparky came back from their walk. They crossed the parking lot to join the kids.

"What's going on?" Debbie asked Parker. "Who moved the Bug?"

"I did," Parker said. "The leopard didn't escape! She was kidnapped! The cops are on their way to arrest the guy and get Jade back!" He grinned at Debbie. "If we hurry, we can get there before she has her baby!"

Debbie looked at Sparky. "Grab your camera!" she said.

Sparky ran for his trailer while Debbie climbed into her van. "Everyone in!" she said.

CHAPTER SIXTEEN

Parker and the three kids jumped into the van, and Debbie drove over to Sparky's trailer. A minute later, he ran out and tossed his equipment into the back. Debbie sped out of the parking lot.

"Where to?" she asked.

"Eight miles down this road!" Dink said. "Look for a mailbox with a wolf's head on it."

Debbie raced the van down the road while Dink tried not to hold his breath. He could feel his heart beating way too fast.

Twelve minutes later, Debbie slowed

and pulled to the right. "There's the mail-box with the wolf's head." She drove into the rutted driveway and stopped.

"The cops don't want us here," Josh said. "They said it's dangerous."

Debbie looked at him. "Why?"

"Because of Jade," Ruth Rose said. "But Dr. Akbar is with the two officers. He said Jade won't try to hurt anyone."

"But we don't even know if Jade is here," Dink said. "We just *think* she is." He explained about Lester and the abandoned house. "Rob Wolff knows Lester, and we think they kidnapped Jade together and brought her here."

"What is here, exactly?" Sparky asked from behind them. "What's at the end of this driveway?"

"Rob lives here," Ruth Rose said. "He has some llamas and chickens, and his vet told us how to get to his house."

"We can't just go barging in, Deb," Sparky said.

Debbie tapped her fingernails on the steering wheel. "Okay, here's a plan," she said after a minute. "Parker, Sparky, and I will walk down the driveway and find the house. If the police are there and so is Jade, I'll try to persuade them to let us film the rescue."

"But what about us?" Josh asked. "We're the ones who figured out that Jade was kidnapped! We showed the cops the first house they kept her in!"

"I know," Debbie said. "But stay in the van for now. I'll try to get the police to let you watch us film. Later, we'll put you in the film with Parker. You'll be heroes, and I'll even pay you!"

"Still not fair," Josh muttered.

"I promise I'll come back and let you know what's happening," Parker said. They all fist-bumped. Then Parker, Debbie, and Sparky left the van and hiked up the driveway.

Minutes passed. The three kids tried

peering through the bushes but couldn't see more than twenty feet ahead of the van.

"Let's just go see if there's a house, at least," Josh said. "We'll be quiet as chipmunks. We'll blend into the trees like we're invisible."

"Officer Diggs will arrest us," Dink said. "He'll put us in jail. No food, just spiders."

"I'm with Josh," Ruth Rose said. "Come on, Dink!"

The three kids slipped out of the van and moved up the driveway. Like chipmunks, they scampered over dirt, weeds, and broken tree branches.

The driveway turned a corner around a big tree. Up ahead, the kids saw a gravel parking space in front of a small yellow house. The police van was parked next to Rob's truck.

"I guess Rob's here," Josh said.

"Shhh," Dink said. "We're chipmunks!"

About a hundred yards to the left of the house stood a small barn. Attached to the barn, a white fence surrounded a small paddock.

Two llamas were standing inside the fence. They were making strange noises and stamping their hooves.

"Now what?" Dink asked.

"Everyone must be in the house," Ruth Rose said.

They sat down between some bushes. "There better not be any spiders in here," Josh said.

Dink giggled. "Chipmunks eat spiders," he said.

They waited and watched the house.

"What's that noise?" Ruth Rose asked.

"I didn't hear anything," Josh said.

Dink sat up, unfolding his legs. "I did," he said.

They peered out of the bushes and saw a bunch of red chickens inside a wire fence. The fence was attached to the barn, and there was a small opening where the chickens could go inside the barn. But they were outside, squawking and flapping their wings.

The llamas continued making the strange noises. They ran from one end of the paddock to the other. Dirt flew up from their hooves as they raced around.

"They look scared," Dink said. "Why

don't they just go inside the barn? The door is wide open."

"The chickens are scared, too," Josh said.

"Something is happening," Ruth Rose whispered. A side door to the house opened. Officers Brown and Diggs came out. Rob Wolff and Lester were with them. The four walked toward the barn.

CHAPTER SEVENTEEN

The kids froze and watched.

Nothing happened. After a few minutes, Officer Brown and Rob left the barn. Lester and Officer Diggs followed, and they all entered the house. The screen door slammed.

The llamas raced back and forth in the paddock.

The chickens were still squawking.

"Something is really bugging them," Josh said.

"It can't be us, or they'd run inside," Ruth Rose said. "It's almost like they're

afraid of the barn. They're staying as far away from it as they can get."

"You're right," Dink said. "Let's go find out what's scaring them. You guys coming with me?"

"Awesome!" Josh said. "I'm tired of being a chipmunk!"

They ran along the outside of the paddock, making sure no one in the house could see them. Then they climbed over the fence and raced into the barn through the wide door.

Even with doors open at both ends, it was dim inside the barn. The kids stood and looked around. Bales of hay were stacked high against one wall. The opposite side had stalls with half doors that swung open. The barn floor was covered with dust and pieces of hay.

"Keep your eyes open for Officer Brown," Josh whispered. "If she finds out we're here, she'll handcuff us."

The kids looked inside each stall.

They were empty except for feed and water. Soft cooing noises came from up in the rafters. They didn't see anything that would frighten llamas.

Six bales of hay were piled in the middle of the floor. Ruth Rose sat on one and looked at the ceiling. Spiderwebs clung to the thick rafters. A row of dusty windows just under the ceiling let in a little light.

"Nothing here but pigeons," she said.

"Watch out for the poop," Josh said. "I mean *scat.*"

Dink went to the door to make sure no one was coming from the yellow house. He started walking back toward Josh and Ruth Rose, then stopped. He bent down and stared at something on the floor.

"Guys, come over here," Dink said. "But walk along the sides, not down the middle."

Josh and Ruth Rose joined Dink in front of the open barn door.

"What are we looking for?" Ruth Rose asked.

"Step out of the way so the sunlight comes in," Dink said. When they moved to one side, Dink pointed at the floor. "Those are tire tracks coming into the barn."

"Rob probably drives his truck in here," Josh said.

"Yeah, but look where the tire marks stop," Dink said. "Those bales are in the way. He'd have to back out instead of driving straight through and out the other door."

The others just looked at him.

"I'm wondering why Rob left those bales in the middle of the floor," Dink said. "Why not stack them against the wall with the rest?"

Dink walked over and kicked at one of the bales. It didn't budge. "Help me move them," he said.

Josh and Ruth Rose grabbed one of

the bales. With the three of them tugging, they were able to slide it to one side.

"Move it more," Dink said. "Something is underneath!"

When they'd shoved all six bales out of the way, the kids found a sheet of plywood hidden beneath them. Dink pulled up one corner and looked down into a black hole.

"It's a secret cellar!" Josh said.

Ruth Rose pulled her flashlight from a backpack pocket. She switched the light on. Then she stuck the flashlight into the hole and lowered her head. When she looked up, her face was white.

"See anything spooky?" Josh asked.

Ruth Rose nodded. "I know what made the llamas and chickens so scared," she said. "Jade is down there!"

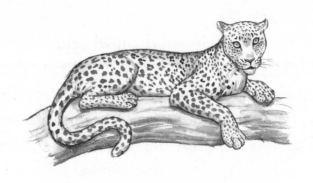

CHAPTER EIGHTEEN

"Is she . . . is she okay?" Dink asked.

"I think so," Ruth Rose said. "She's in some kind of cage. I saw her green eyes looking at me!"

"We'd better get Dr. Akbar!" Josh said.

"But he's in the house with Rob and Sofi's brother," Dink said. "And I'm pretty sure they're the kidnappers!"

"I have an idea." Ruth Rose found a pencil and paper in her backpack. She wrote something on the paper. "You and I will go in the house," she said. "I'll tell

Dr. Akbar that Josh got hurt and needs his help. You give my note to one of the officers."

"They'll be mad that we didn't stay at the zoo," Josh said.

"But they'll forgive us when they read that," Ruth Rose said.

"What's it say?" Josh asked.

She read it out loud:

WE FOUND JADE.
COME TO THE BARN.

"Okay, let's do it!" Dink said. He and Ruth Rose headed for the house. Dink opened the door, and they stepped inside.

The two officers were standing in the kitchen, talking to Rob Wolff and Lester French. Dr. Akbar was leaning against the sink. Parker, Debbie, and Sparky were sitting at the table, waiting for something to happen. They all gawked when Dink and Ruth Rose walked in.

Before anyone could say anything, Ruth Rose ran up to Dr. Akbar. "Josh cut his finger on something sharp in the barn!" she cried. "He's bleeding!"

While everyone was staring at Ruth Rose, Dink stepped in front of Officer Brown. With his hand behind his back, he wiggled the note so she would notice it. He felt the note being plucked from his fingers as Dr. Akbar grabbed his bag and rushed out the door behind Ruth Rose.

Lester and Rob were staring at Dink. "Don't I know you?" Rob Wolff asked.

Dink's mouth was too dry to answer.

"Well, I know him," Sofi's brother said. "He was sneaking around my place with that girl and another kid!"

Lester lunged for Dink, but he stopped when Officer Diggs stepped between them. "Whoa there," he said, reaching for his handcuffs.

Dink bolted out of the kitchen. He tore across the yard, straight for the barn door. When he got there, Dr. Akbar was already on his knees peering inside the hidden space.

He looked up with a smile. "Jade seems fine!" he said. "She's even purring!"

Just then, Officer Diggs walked into the barn, followed by Parker, Debbie, and Sparky. Officer Diggs shook his head at Josh. "How's that bleeding?" he asked.

Josh blushed and held up both hands, wiggling his fingers. "All better," he said. "It's a miracle!"

"Okay, Rob and his pal Lester told us the whole plot. We're taking them to the station," Officer Diggs said, nodding at the hole. "Is your leopard down there?"

"Yes, and she seems in good shape," Dr. Akbar said. "I'll examine her once she's back in her own space."

Officer Diggs bent over and looked in the hole. "How are you going to get her out?" he asked.

"I've already called the zoo," Dr. Akbar said. "They're bringing a small crane that should be able to lift that cage."

"This is excellent!" Debbie said. "Let's set up, Sparky."

"Not too close to the hole," Dr. Akbar said. "The truck has to get in here. And

we may have to cut a bigger opening in this floor."

Officer Diggs smiled. "I don't think Mr. Wolff will notice," he said. "Those three kidnappers have other things to think about."

"*Three* kidnappers?" Ruth Rose asked.

"Yeah, Sofi is the third," he said. "The two in the house ratted her out. It was Sofi French's idea to kidnap a rare, endangered animal for ransom. She mixed some sleeping pills into a few of those fancy meatballs and convinced her brother to use his drone to drop them into Jade's enclosure."

Dink grinned at Josh. "Just like you said, Fred."

Josh tapped his head. "It's the Josh brain, Wayne."

Officer Diggs looked at his watch. "Sofi will be driving to Flip's gas station, looking for the ransom, anytime now," he said. "We have a cruiser waiting for her."

Just then, a flatbed truck pulled up outside the barn. Three men jumped out of the cab and began unloading a small crane. Dr. Akbar explained the situation, and the men went to work.

Two of them used iron pry bars to rip away the wood flooring, making the opening wider. The third guy drove the crane up to the hole.

Parker and the kids sat on hay bales. They watched Dr. Akbar climb into the hole, dragging a chain attached to a big steel hook. A few minutes later, his head popped up. "Okay, just pull the cage toward the opening," he said.

One of the workers gave him a hand, and he climbed onto the barn floor. The crane operator backed up slowly. The chain straightened, and the kids could hear the cage being dragged.

When the cage was under the hole, the crane guy ran over to help the others. It took four men, but finally the cage

was out of the hole and resting on the floor. Jade was crouched inside, hissing and showing her teeth to the men.

Dr. Akbar took a meatball from a baggie and fed it to Jade. "You'll be home in a few minutes," he told her. "Your friends are waiting for you."

Once the crane was back on the flatbed, the men placed the cage behind it and lashed it down with ropes. Dr. Akbar climbed up and sat next to the cage. Jade licked his fingers through the bars.

The flatbed backed out of the barn, turned, and headed down the driveway.

"Well, that's a first for me," Officer Diggs said. "I've rescued little old ladies, babies, and kittens, but never a pregnant leopard!"

He looked at Parker and the kids. "Officer Brown is staying here till our backup comes, but I'll give you folks a ride home."

Dink looked at his watch. "Perfect," he said. "It's almost noon. My dad will be waiting for us."

"A pistachio ice cream cone is waiting for me!" Josh said.

Parker made a face. "My laptop will be waiting for me," he said. Then he grinned. "Maybe I'll change my story to a different kind of kidnapping!"

CHAPTER NINETEEN

The next morning, Dink's father drove the kids to the zoo. Parker was waiting for them at the entrance with his special pass. They all hiked along the path to Jade's enclosure.

Dr. Akbar smiled when he saw them. He held up two thumbs. Debbie and Sparky were already filming. The enclosure was empty.

"Where's Jade?" Dink asked.

"She's in the cave, nursing her two beautiful cubs," Dr. Akbar said quietly. "The camera is paired to my phone."

He held his phone so they could see

the screen. The kids huddled together, and Dink's father looked over their heads. At first, all they saw was darkness. Then they saw Jade.

Next to her tummy were two tiny Amur leopards. Their fur was golden-colored, and their eyes were shut tight. As they nursed from their mother, their little tails wiggled.

"They are so awesome!" Josh said.

"Like little kittens!" Ruth Rose said.

"Mom and cubs all look happy and healthy," Dr. Akbar said. "Thanks to you kids, Jade gave birth in her own cave, not in some cage hidden under a barn floor."

"When can we film the babies?" Debbie asked.

"In about two weeks, they'll be crawling and their fur will start to grow spots," Dr. Akbar said. "Momma Jade will bring them out to get sunlight."

"Do they have names yet?" Ruth Rose asked.

Dr. Akbar smiled. "Our team is going over some Russian and Chinese names," he said. "We don't know yet if the cubs are boys or girls or one of each."

"Joshua is a nice name for a leopard," Josh said.

Everyone laughed.

"How about if I treat us all to breakfast?" Dink's father said.

"Can we have ice cream?" Josh asked.

"You three are heroes," Mr. Duncan said. "You can have anything you want!"

All three kids yelled and fist-bumped.

"And I might even forgive you for scaring me to death yesterday," Mr. Duncan added, "when you came back to the motel in a police cruiser!"

DID YOU FIND THE
SECRET MESSAGE
HIDDEN IN THIS BOOK?

If you *don't* want
to know the answer,
don't look at the bottom
of this page!

Answer:
WHAT SHOULD JADE'S CUBS BE NAMED?

GET THE FACTS FROM A TO Z!

To learn more about the facts in this mystery, find these books at your local library or bookstore:

Books About San Diego

Class Trip: San Diego by Kathleen Tracy (Mitchell Lane, 2010)

The Tree Lady: The True Story of How One Tree-Loving Woman Changed a City Forever by H. Joseph Hopkins, illustrated by Jill McElmurry (Beach Lane, 2013)

Books About the San Diego Zoo

My Book of Wild Animals by San Diego Zoo (Ideals, 2007)

Who Pooped in the Zoo? Exploring the Weirdest, Wackiest, Grossest & Most Surprising Facts About Zoo Poop by Caroline Patterson, illustrated by Robert Rath (Farcountry, 2007)

Books About Leopards

The Great Leopard Rescue: Saving the Amur Leopards by Sandra Markle (Millbrook, 2016)

A Leap for Legadema: The True Story of a Little Leopard in a Big World by Beverly and Dereck Joubert (National Geographic, 2018)
Leopards by Claire Throp (Heinemann, 2014)

Books About Drones

Drones: Science, Technology, Engineering by Steven Otfinoski (Children's Press, 2016)
Robots and Drones: Past, Present, and Future by Mairghread Scott (First Second, 2018)

Books About Animals

The Fascinating Animal Book for Kids: 500 Wild Facts! by Ginjer L. Clarke (Rockridge, 2020)
Zoology for Kids: Understanding and Working with Animals by Josh and Bethanie Hestermann, with a foreword by the Kratt brothers (Chicago Review, 2015)